Mary-in-Middle

By Sandy Asher

Illustrated by
Mark Alan Weatherby

A
LITTLE APPLE
PAPERBACK

SCHOLASTIC INC.
New York Toronto London Auckland Sydney

For Joan Kunsch

ISBN 0-590-43836-0

Copyright © 1990 by Sandy Asher
Illustrations copyright © 1990 by Scholastic Inc.
All rights reserved. Published by Scholastic Inc.
APPLE PAPERBACKS is a registered trademark of Scholastic Inc.

12 11 10 9 8 7 6 5 4 3   0 1 2 3 4 5/9

Printed in the U.S.A.   40
First Scholastic printing, November 1990

CONTENTS

Other books in the Ballet One series:

**#1 Best Friends Get Better
#2 Pat's Promise**

Chapter One
One Potato, Two Potato

"One potato, two potato," Mary Stone sang. "Three potato, *four*. Five potato, six potato, seven potato, *more*."

She tapped Pat Parker's right fist, then her left. She tapped Ellie Bell's fists, one at a time, and then her own. Round and round she went, from Pat to Ellie to herself.

"I'm out," she said at last. "I'll sleep on the floor."

"It has to be Pat or me," Ellie said. "It's your house. You have to sleep in the bed with the one who wins."

"That's right," Pat agreed.

It was the first thing the two of them had agreed on all evening. But it didn't make sense.

Mary unrolled the sleeping bag. She spread it out on the floor beside her bed. "Whoever lost 'One Potato, Two Potato' has to sleep on the floor. That's me."

She fluffed her pillow and dropped it on the sleeping bag. Ellie and Pat gave each other unhappy looks.

Mary sighed. Ellie and Pat were her best friends. That was why she had invited them to spend Friday night at her house. But ever since they'd arrived, the two of them had done nothing but fight. Mary felt like the rope in a tug-of-war.

"All right," she said. "We'll do 'One Potato, Two Potato' again. Just between the two of you."

Pat and Ellie put up their fists. Mary

sang the song again. This time, Pat lost.

Pat shook her head so hard, her two yellow bunches of curls flapped like dog ears. "I'm not sleeping on the floor," she said.

"But you lost!" Ellie yelped. "It was fair and square."

"I'm not sleeping on the floor," Pat said again. Her round face scrunched up in an angry pout.

"Oh, Pat, why not?" Mary asked. She was beginning to think nobody would ever get to sleep anywhere. They would just stay awake all night, fighting.

Pat folded her arms. "I'm just not," she said.

"You *have* to!" Ellie insisted. She poked her glasses up on her nose and frowned hard at Pat. "You *lost*, Pat."

Pat plopped down on the edge of Mary's bed. Her eyes filled with tears.

"Don't cry, Pat," Mary said. "And stop yelling at her, Ellie."

"But she lost!" Ellie snapped.

"I don't care!" Pat shouted.

"OH, CAN'T YOU TWO EVER STOP FIGHTING?"

Ellie and Pat both looked at Mary, their eyes wide with surprise. Mary almost never yelled. She was always the one who tried to patch things up.

"I thought it was going to be so much fun having you spend the night," she said sadly.

Ellie looked ashamed. "Me, too," she said.

Pat sniffled. "Me, too," she said.

Mary smiled at them both hopefully. "We still have all night," she said. "And all tomorrow morning. And lunch. Then we go to Ballet One together. It could still be fun."

Ellie and Pat nodded their heads.

"But you have to stop fighting," Mary reminded them.

"Okay," Ellie said. "No more fighting. Now, you lost 'One Potato, Two Potato,' " she said to Pat, "so you have to do what we said."

"I am not sleeping on the floor," Pat insisted.

"You *have* to!" Ellie shouted.

There was a knock on the door. "Keep it down, please," called Mary's father.

Mary took a deep breath. "I'll sleep on the floor," she said. "I really don't mind."

"*No!*" said Pat.

"*No!*" said Ellie.

"Why not?" asked Mary.

"Because I don't want you to," said Pat.

Mary couldn't believe her ears. "Why *not*?" she asked.

"I know why!" Ellie broke in. She squinted

at Pat angrily. "She wants *me* to sleep on the floor. She wants you two together and me all by myself."

Pat blushed a deep red and pressed her lips shut.

Ellie did a furious dance around the bed. She stomped her feet and waved her arms. "You're not playing fair, Pat Parker!" she cried.

Just then, Mary's stepmother opened the bedroom door and peeked in. "You'll have to keep your voices down, girls," she said. "The little boys are trying to sleep in the next room."

The "little boys" were Mary's younger brothers, Tony and Billy. Tony was three years old, and Billy was a year and a half. The "big boys" were Mary's older brothers, Josh and Zach. Josh was fourteen, and Zach was twelve.

Mary was the only girl. She was almost

nine, and tall for her age, taller than Ellie and Pat. But she was right in the middle of her family—not little and not big.

"Okay," Mary said, lowering her voice to a whisper.

Her stepmother smiled. "Thanks, Mary," she said. "Good night, girls."

"Good night, Mrs. Stone," whispered Pat and Ellie.

But as soon as Mrs. Stone was gone, the fight started again.

Chapter Two
Mashed Potatoes

"You'll tell secrets," Pat whispered, "while I'm all by myself on the floor."

"We will not!" Ellie hissed. "That's silly."

"You will," Pat said. "You'll probably even tell secrets about *me*."

"There's only one secret about you," Ellie said, her voice growing louder again. "*You don't play fair.* And that's no secret."

"Well, I can't help it," Pat wailed. "It's no fun being all alone while everyone else tells secrets."

"Stop talking about secrets!" Ellie shouted

9

at her. "There *aren't* any dumb secrets."

"Shhhh!" Mary warned them.

Too late. In the next room, Billy howled.

"Mama! Mama!" Tony called. "Billy's crying!" And he began crying, too, even louder than Billy.

The girls got very quiet. Mary held her breath. The door to her room opened again. This time, Mrs. Stone was not smiling. She gave Mary a dark look. "If I have to come in one more time," she said, "you will all sleep in different rooms."

"Sorry," Mary said. "We'll be quiet. Really."

Ellie and Pat nodded. "Sorry," they said.

Mrs. Stone closed the door. The girls waited. In a few minutes, all was peaceful again in the next room.

"Okay," Mary said softly. "Here's what we'll do. We'll *all* sleep in the bed."

"There isn't room," Ellie said. "We'll be squashed."

Mary looked at the small bed. Then she looked at Ellie and Pat. "I'll sleep in the middle," she offered.

"Okay," Ellie and Pat agreed.

Pat jumped off the bed and helped Mary roll up the sleeping bag. They tucked it way back in the closet. Ellie lined up three pillows on the bed.

Then they all hopped in, giggling. Ellie and Pat turned off the lamps on the night tables next to the bed. The room got dark and quiet.

"Good night," Mary said.

"No secrets?" Pat asked.

"I don't know any secrets," said Mary.

"Told you there weren't any," Ellie said. "How about some ghost stories?"

"No!" said Pat. "I don't like ghost stories."

"Scaredy-cat," Ellie said.

"Ellie, stop it," Mary said.

11

"I can't help it," Pat said. "Ghost stories give me nightmares."

"No secrets, no ghost stories," said Mary.

"No nothing," muttered Ellie.

"This sure isn't as much fun as I thought it would be," said Pat.

Mary was thinking the exact same thing. But what could she do?

For a minute, no one said a word. Then Mary felt Pat take a deep breath beside her.

"Okay," Pat said. "Maybe one ghost story."

"All right!" Ellie squealed. "And maybe one secret."

"What?" Pat asked.

"Ghost stories kind of give me night-mares, too," Ellie admitted.

Mary threw the blanket over her head and sat up slowly. "Wooooo-oooooo-ooooooooo!" she softly moaned.

Ellie and Pat shrieked and pulled her down.

"Shhhh!" she warned them. "Scream *quietly*."

They whispered and giggled until Pat and Ellie fell asleep. Pat snored softly into her pillow. Ellie mumbled as she slept.

Mary wanted to turn over. But she didn't want to wake the others up. Oh, well, she thought, there isn't enough room to turn over, anyway.

She lay awake a long time, listening to Ellie mumble and Pat snore. Her arms and legs were falling asleep, but at least they were all friends again.

"One potato, two potato," she whispered to herself in the dark. "Three potatoes, *mashed*."

Chapter Three
Exciting News

"Let's fix each other's hair for Ballet One," Mary said first thing Saturday morning.

Ballet One wasn't until after lunch. But just thinking about it always made Mary feel good. "We could all wear our hair up in buns, like Miss Drew," she said. "You want to?"

"Okay," said Pat.

"Okay," said Ellie.

Soon they were busy with brushes and barrettes. They swept each other's hair back, the way their teacher wore hers. They talked about Ballet One.

Except for one little fight about whose hair to fix first, Ellie and Pat were getting along today. Mary smiled as she checked her own hair in the mirror. Ballet One always made everyone feel better.

After lunch, Mr. Stone drove them to the South Oaks Shopping Center. He dropped them off in front of Miss Drew's School of Dance.

"Hello, girls!" Miss Drew called, as they hurried inside the big, bright room. "Let's hurry and get started. I've got exciting news for you today."

"What is it?" Mary asked.

Miss Drew smiled her pretty smile. "Not now," she said. "I'll tell you after our *barre* work. Get your ballet slippers on."

Paul Dobbs and his little brother, Stanley, were already at the *barre*. They were practicing the step they'd all learned last week: *ronds de jambe*. They made half circles on the floor with their toes: front, side, back, front, side, back.

"Do you know what Miss Drew's surprise is?" Mary asked them.

Paul shook his head. Stanley said, "Nope."

Nancy and Sarah sat in the corner, changing their shoes. They didn't know what the surprise was, either.

Lynn and Rosa rushed in, late and out of breath. They yanked off the jeans and sweatshirts they wore over their leotards.

"Miss Drew has exciting news," Mary told them. "But nobody knows what it is."

Soon the whole room was buzzing with questions about Miss Drew's secret. Not even Mr. Ross, who played the piano for their class, knew what it was.

"Please tell us," Mary begged Miss Drew.

"Pretty, pretty, *pretty* please?" said Pat.

"With whipped cream and chocolate sprinkles and a cherry on top?" added Ellie.

Miss Drew just laughed and called them all to the *barre*. Mr. Ross struck up the music for *pliés,* and class began.

Barre work seemed to last forever. They'd learned a lot of new steps since September. Harder steps, too. Mary's legs were getting tired. She could barely keep her arms up. But she tried her very best to do everything right. She wanted to dance just like Miss Drew.

"Straight backs," Miss Drew said. "And bring your foot all the way around on your *ronds de jambe*. Mary's got it. Show the class, Mary."

The class turned and looked at Mary. Mr. Ross played the *ronds de jambe* music again. Mary moved her foot slowly—front, side, back, front. She tried hard to keep her back straight and her head up.

"Very nice, Mary," Miss Drew said. "Now you try it, class."

Mary was glad to have everyone dancing again. Miss Drew often chose her to show steps to the class. But it still made her nervous to have them all watching her.

At last, it was time for the last *barre* exercise: *grands battements*. Mr. Ross played loud chords on the piano. Mary kicked her legs as high as she could: to the front, to the side, to the back, to the side.

19

"Come to the center," Miss Drew said, when the last kick was done.

Everyone gathered around, eager to hear the news.

"All right," Miss Drew said. "This is it. The Springfield Ballet Company is going to do the *Nutcracker* ballet for the very first time this year."

"I saw the *Nutcracker* ballet in Kansas City last year," Pat said. "It was beautiful!"

"Yes, it is," Miss Drew agreed. "And it calls for a lot of dancers. All the ballet students in the area are invited to audition."

"Us, too?" asked Ellie.

"Us, too," said Miss Drew. "At the end of class, I'll hand out notes for you to take home to your families. This will be a real ballet on a real stage, with wonderful music, costumes, and scenery. The finest dancers in the area will be in it."

"But we're just beginners," Mary said. More than anything in the whole world, she wanted to be in that ballet. But how was it possible?

"That's all right," Miss Drew said. "They need lots of children. You'll have to get your parents' permission, though. A parent will have to come to the audition with each of you to get all the information. It takes time and hard work to put on a ballet. You'll have to attend many rehearsals and every performance."

Mary didn't mind the hard work one bit. But bringing a parent—that was going to be a problem. Hers were always so busy!

"I know my mom will let me," said Pat.

"Mine, too," said Ellie.

They turned toward Mary.

"Your parents will let you, won't they?" Pat asked.

Mary didn't answer.

"Sure they will," Ellie answered for her.

But Mary wasn't so sure.

Chapter Four
Too Little, Too Big

Mrs. Stone picked Mary up after Ballet One. Billy and Tony were in the backseat. Mary hopped into the front, beside her stepmother.

"Ellie and Pat have rides home, don't they?" Mrs. Stone asked.

"They're already gone," Mary said. She had Miss Drew's note in her mittened hand. "Mom—" she began.

"Oh, good," Mrs. Stone went on. "Then we don't have to drop them off." She backed the station wagon out of its parking spot. "I'm already running late."

Mary liked it when her parents were late picking her up from Ballet One. Miss Drew's next Saturday class was Ballet Five. They were the best dancers in the school. Mary loved to watch them warm up. Miss Drew said if Mary worked hard, she would be a Ballet Five someday.

"I've got to get Tony to the doctor by three-fifteen," Mrs. Stone said. "He has a sore throat."

"Why did you bring Billy?" Mary asked.

"There's nobody home to watch him," Mrs. Stone said. "Josh is raking a neighbor's leaves. Zach is at Sally's house. They're working on their science fair project. And Daddy is at the service station. His car broke down again."

"I can watch Billy," Mary said.

"Thank you, Mary," Mrs. Stone said. "I always know I can count on you."

"Can I watch him at home?" asked Mary.

"No, you'll have to do it at the doctor's office. You're still too young to baby-sit at home alone. And I don't have time to drop you off, anyway."

"Okay," Mary said.

She tucked Miss Drew's note into her jacket pocket. It would wait until her parents weren't so busy. She turned around to look at her little brothers.

Billy was asleep, his head flopped down on his chest. Tony was wide awake. His chubby face was flushed with fever. His dark eyes were red and watery from crying.

"Does your throat hurt bad, Tony?" Mary asked.

Tony pushed his bottom lip out and nodded.

"I'm sorry," Mary said. "How about if I read you a bunch of stories when we get home?"

Tony loved stories. He nodded again, a

little faster. But he didn't seem much happier.

Mrs. Stone got stuck in a left turn lane. "Oh, no," she said. "We'll never get there on time." Finally the light changed. She sped around the corner.

That woke Billy up. He started to cry.

"Not now, Billy," Mrs. Stone begged. "Please not now. We'll be at Dr. Harris's office in five minutes. She has lots of toys in her waiting room, remember? And Mary will play with you there."

"We'll play horsey," Mary offered.

Billy stopped crying right away. "Horsey!" he said.

"No, not horsey," Mrs. Stone told him. "Toys."

"Horsey!" Billy said.

"Josh and Zach play horsey with him all the time," Mary said.

"Josh and Zach are strong enough to

hold him up," Mrs. Stone said. "You might get hurt."

"I'm strong," said Mary. "Miss Drew says I have a good, strong, dancer's body."

"No horsey," said Mrs. Stone. "That's all we need now—a couple of good, strong, broken bones."

"Okay," said Mary. "No horsey."

Billy started crying again.

A minute later, Mrs. Stone pulled up in front of Dr. Harris's office. "Unbuckle Billy," she told Mary. She was already out of the car and unbuckling Tony's seat belt.

Mary worked Billy's straps and buckles loose. Then she helped him out of the car. Mrs. Stone scooped him up in one arm. She held on to Tony with her other hand. Mary hurried into the office building behind them.

Billy liked the ride on his mother's hip. By the time they got to Dr. Harris's waiting room, he was in a good mood. He ran to the pile of blocks in the corner and sat down to play.

But Tony wasn't happy. "It hurts," he said.

Mary felt sorry for him. "There are books here," she said. "I'll read to you until Dr. Harris is ready to see you. Okay?"

"No," said Tony. "I want Mommy."

He crawled onto Mrs. Stone's lap. He buried his face against her shoulder. Mrs. Stone rocked him in her arms.

Mary felt left out. She knew Tony didn't mean to make her feel that way. He was just a three-year-old. And he was sick. But she felt left out just the same.

She wondered how it felt to be cuddled in your mother's lap.

Mary couldn't remember her first mother. She had died when Mary was only two. Mary was four when her stepmother came. Four was little enough to crawl into a lap, she thought. But she remembered feeling too shy to do it. She felt shy with her stepmother for a long time. And now, she guessed she was too big for crawling into laps.

Mary took off her jacket and hat. She hung them up on a giraffe coatrack. Miss Drew's note stuck out of her pocket. Mary pulled it out and unfolded it.

"Mom—" she said.

A white door at the end of the waiting room opened. A nurse stepped out. "Mrs. Stone?" she said. "The doctor will see Tony now."

"Thank you," said Mrs. Stone. "Keep an eye on Billy, Mary." She and Tony disappeared through the white door.

Mary put the note away again. She sat on the floor beside Billy. She built towers of blocks for him. He knocked them down. Every time the blocks toppled and fell, he laughed and said, "More!"

I'm too big for blocks, Mary thought. And too little to baby-sit alone at home. Too big to crawl onto Mom's lap, like Tony. Too little to rake leaves for money, like Josh. Too big to ride when the boys play horsey. Too little to be the horse.

"Too big, too little, too little, too big," she said. That made Billy laugh, too.

"It's not funny, Billy," Mary told him. "Mary-in-the-middle, that's me. And the middle isn't any place at all."

Chapter Five
Busy, Busy, Busy

"How's Tony?" asked Mr. Stone.

Mary, Mrs. Stone, and the little boys had just gotten home from the doctor's office. Mr. Stone was in the kitchen. He was making chicken soup for dinner.

"We've got some medicine," Mrs. Stone said. "He'll be fine. How's the car?"

"It's old," Mr. Stone said. "But it'll be fine, too. For a while. I hope."

Mary took her coat off and hung it up in the closet. She slipped Miss Drew's note out of the pocket. She put it on the dinner table next to her plate. Then she helped the big boys set the table.

"We'd better start shopping for a new car, though," Mr. Stone went on.

"When?" Mrs. Stone asked. "We don't have a minute to spare. We seem to be driving children around twenty-four hours a day. We drive to nursery school, regular school, ballet, scout meetings, PTA—"

"The doctor's office," Mr. Stone reminded her, "and the service station to fix the old car."

"You left out basketball practice," Josh said. "I'll be getting out of school too late for the bus from now on. Somebody will have to pick me up."

"What about me?" Zach asked. "Sally and I have two weeks to finish our science project. Her dad can't do all the driving."

"We'll handle it," Mr. Stone said. "Right now, let's eat. We all need our strength!"

Mrs. Stone served the soup. She noticed the paper next to Mary's bowl. "What's that, Mary?" she asked.

"Oh, it's—" Mary began.

Splat! Billy's spoon hit his soup and splashed it all over his high-chair tray.

"Oh, no!" said Mrs. Stone, and ran into the kitchen for a towel.

Mary tossed Miss Drew's note under the table. She scooped up a spoonful of soup. Voices buzzed around her head as she ate. "If Sally and I win the local science fair," Zach said, "we get to go to the state fair in Jefferson City. A parent has to go with us. Her dad can't get off work."

"We'll handle it," Mrs. Stone said, mopping up Billy's mess.

"Parkview could go to the state championships this year," Josh said. "Coach says we're the strongest team he's worked with."

"We'll go to all the games, won't we, Dad?" Zach asked.

"As many as we have time for," Mr. Stone said.

Mary put down her spoon. Suddenly she didn't feel very hungry. Every time someone at the table spoke, her family got busier and busier.

After dinner, she took Miss Drew's note up to her room, without showing it to anybody. She hid it in her old toy box. No one would want to drive her to the audition and all those rehearsals and performances. No one *could*. They were just too busy.

Mary sat down on her bed and sighed. She was too little to drive herself to the *Nutcracker* ballet. And she was too big to cry.

Chapter Six
Mary-Left-Out

"It never hurts to ask," Pat said. "That's what my mom always says."

It was Monday morning. Mary, Pat, and Ellie were in the school yard. They stood near the wall, away from the wind. It was recess time. But it was too cold to play.

Pat and Ellie wanted to talk about the *Nutcracker* ballet. They both had permission to audition. They couldn't understand why Mary hadn't even asked her parents about it.

"I just couldn't ask," Mary explained.

"Everyone was too busy. Tony had a sore throat on Saturday. Then Billy got sick on Sunday. And my dad's car broke down again."

"But you will ask, won't you?" Ellie said.

"I'm not sure," Mary said.

"You *have* to!" Pat told her.

"*Tonight!*" Ellie added.

"What's all the excitement about?" It was Mr. Crane, their third-grade teacher. He wore a bright yellow scarf around his neck. His nose was red from the cold.

"We're auditioning for the *Nutcracker* ballet," Pat said.

"That *is* exciting," Mr. Crane said. "Where? When?"

"Next Monday night," Pat told him. "At the Landers Theater. They need lots of extra dancers."

"When I lived in St. Louis," Mr. Crane said, "people who had never taken a single dance class got to be in the *Nutcracker* ballet. They played guests in a party scene."

"Were you in it, Mr. Crane?" Ellie asked.

"No, but I saw it," Mr. Crane said. "I've always thought it would be fun to be in a ballet."

Ralph Major and David Sims galloped up.

Ralph crashed right into Ellie. "Ballet? Yuck!" he said. Then he stuck his finger into his mouth. He pretended to throw up.

"Oh, will you stop that, Ralph?" Ellie told him. "Every time somebody says 'ballet,' you do the same thing. Can't you think of anything new?"

"Every time I look at you, you're ugly," said Ralph. "Can't *you* think of anything new?"

"Third-graders," said Mr. Crane, "if you can't think of anything nice to say, button your lips."

Ralph pretended to button about a hundred buttons on his lips. Mr. Crane frowned at him until he stopped. Then he walked away to check on the rest of the class.

"What's a *Nutcracker* ballet, anyway?" Ralph asked. "A ballet for nuts?"

"Quit it, Ralph," David said. Then he turned toward Ellie. "What *is* a *Nutcracker* ballet?"

37

Ellie shrugged and looked at Mary. "I saw pictures in a book," she said. "But I'm still not sure what it is."

Mary didn't know, either. She'd never thought about it. She just wanted to be in a real ballet, whatever it was. She looked at Pat, who was wearing a big grin.

"*I* know," Pat said. "Last year, my mom and I went to Kansas City. We stayed at a big hotel—"

"Recess is almost over," David reminded her.

"Okay," Pat said. "So we saw the *Nutcracker* ballet. It was like a play, only people danced instead of talking."

"Dumb," said Ralph. "Couldn't they speak English?"

"Dancers aren't supposed to talk," Ellie told him.

"There's this girl named Clara," Pat went on. "Her uncle gives her a nutcracker for

38

Christmas. It's big, like a doll. She loves it. But her bratty brother breaks it."

"Good," Ralph said.

Pat ignored him. "But it's magic, the Nutcracker," she said. "It comes to life. And a giant Mouse King with seven heads tries to capture it."

"Seven heads!" David said.

Even Ralph said, "Wow!"

"The Mouse King has a bunch of mice in his army," Pat said. "But the Nutcracker has wooden soldiers that come to life, too. There's a big battle. With swords. And rifles. And a cannon."

"Pow!" Ralph yelled. "Ka-boom! Crash!"

Everybody looked at him. His face turned bright red. "Probably all fake stuff," he said quickly.

"Of course it's fake," Pat said. "It's like a play. Anyway, Clara kills the Mouse King with her shoe. And the Nutcracker turns into a prince. He takes her to a magical kingdom where everybody dances for them."

"I knew it would end up dumb," Ralph said.

"It's not dumb," Ellie insisted.

"It sounds like fun," David said.

"It does," Mary agreed. It sounded like so much fun, it made her feel worse than ever about missing it.

"Well, the stuff about the battle was pretty good," Ralph admitted.

"That's the part with the most children," Pat said. "The first part, not the magical kingdom. There are Clara's friends at the Christmas party. And her brother's friends. And the mice and soldiers are children, too."

"I want to fight on the Nutcracker's side," Ellie said. "I want to be a wooden soldier."

"I'd rather be one of Clara's friends,"

Pat said. "You get to wear a beautiful dress and go to the party."

"What about being Clara?" Ellie asked.

"That's a very big part," Pat said.

Mr. Crane blew his whistle.

Ralph and David ran to line up. Ellie and Pat hooked their arms together and walked after them.

"Clara's kind of the star," Pat explained. "The *child* star. The Sugar Plum Fairy is the real star. It's her magical kingdom. But she's a grown-up. I'd like to be Clara. But I'm not good enough yet."

"Me, neither, I guess," said Ellie. "We're only in Ballet One."

"Yes, but you're a good dancer," Pat pointed out.

"Thanks," Ellie said. "You are, too."

"Thanks," said Pat.

Arm in arm, they walked back to class.

41

Mary trailed behind them. She was glad Ellie and Pat were acting like best friends again.

But now, instead of Mary-in-the-middle, she was Mary-left-out.

Chapter Seven
Sometimes Dancers Talk

"More!" Billy said.

He and Mary were sitting on the floor in the living room. They were playing the block game again. Mary built a tower. Billy knocked it down.

Billy was feeling better today. But Mrs. Stone was back at Dr. Harris's office with Tony. Now his ear hurt. Mary wasn't babysitting alone. The big boys were in charge until Mr. and Mrs. Stone got home.

Mary tried to build a new tower. But Billy knocked it down after the third block.

"More!" he yelled. Then he laughed, as if he had told a joke.

Mary sighed. "You have to let me build it up first, Billy," she said. "It's not fair to knock it down so fast."

She put a green block on top of a blue one. Billy smacked them both away. "More!" he said.

"This is dumb," Mary told him. "How about if I dance for you?"

Billy clapped his hands. Mary lifted him onto the sofa. "You be the audience," she said. "I'll dance. You clap your hands."

She put a record on the stereo. It wasn't the *Nutcracker* ballet, but she pretended it was.

"Make believe this is the magical kingdom, Billy," she said. "I'm the Sugar Plum Fairy. I'm dancing for the Prince and Clara, okay? I'm the star."

Billy clapped his hands and laughed.

"That's all I'm going to say to you now," Mary told him. "Dancers don't talk. They dance."

Mary listened to the music. Then she tried to do a Sugar Plum Fairy kind of dance. Since the Sugar Plum Fairy was the grown-up star, Mary danced the hardest steps she knew: *balancé*—the waltz step. *Chaîné* turns—tiny spins across the floor in a long chain. She even tried the steps she saw the Ballet Fives practicing.

Just as she finished *grands jetés*—a line of leaps across the floor—she saw her parents in the doorway. They were watching her. She stopped dancing. The music played on without her.

"Go on, Mary," Mrs. Stone said. "You were doing so well."

Mary shook her head.

"Why not?" asked her father. "You always dance for us. What's wrong?"

"I'm tired," Mary said. "And I have homework to do."

She ran upstairs and flopped down on her bed. She buried her face in her pillow.

She couldn't dance for her parents. Not today. They would ask what her dance was about. She'd have to tell them about the *Nutcracker* ballet. And they'd have to tell her she couldn't audition.

She didn't want to hear that. Even though she already knew it, she didn't want to hear it out loud. "It never hurts to ask," Pat told her. But it *does*, Mary thought. Sometimes it *does* hurt to ask.

Mr. Stone came into Mary's room. He sat down on the edge of her bed. "Tell me what's wrong, Mary," he said.

Mary didn't say a word. She just couldn't.

"Something's been bothering you for days," Mr. Stone went on. "I noticed how quiet you were all weekend. I didn't ask why because the little boys and the car were taking up all of our time. And I thought you would tell me when you were ready."

Mary kept her head smashed into her pillow. It was hard to breathe. But it kept her from crying, too.

"Mary, I want you to sit up," said Mr. Stone. "I want you to look at me and tell me what's wrong."

Mary sat up. She didn't look at her father, though. She looked at the worn spot on the knee of her jeans.

"It's nothing," she said, in a tiny voice. "I can't tell you. Please don't make me tell you."

Just then, Mrs. Stone rushed into the room. She was holding a newspaper.

"Look at this!" she said, pointing at the paper. "The Springfield Ballet Company is holding auditions for the *Nutcracker* ballet. Did you know about this, Mary?"

Now Mary had both of her parents waiting for an answer. There was no way out of it. She pointed at her toy box. "Look in there," she said.

Mrs. Stone opened the toy box. She took out Miss Drew's note and read it. "Why didn't you tell us?" she asked. "Don't you want to be in the ballet?"

"I *do* want to," Mary said. "But someone has to drive me to the audition on Monday. And to the rehearsals and performances after that. You're too busy with the little boys and the big boys. I couldn't ask."

Mrs. Stone sat down on the bed, across from Mr. Stone. "Mary," she said, "the big boys *ask* us to do things for them. So do the little boys, mostly by crying. What makes you think *you* can't ask?"

"Because I'm Mary-in-the-middle," Mary said. Her voice was so low she could hardly hear it herself.

49

"What does that mean?" Mr. Stone asked.

"Josh and Zach have important *big* places to go—like baby-sitting jobs and science fairs. Billy and Tony have important *little* places to go—like the doctor because they're sick. I'm too little to be big and too big to be little."

"I see," said Mrs. Stone. "That does make it hard to know where you fit in." She put her arms around Mary and pulled her close. "Let me tell you something, Mary-in-the-middle. You fit in just fine. Tight and snug."

The next thing Mary knew, she was in her stepmother's lap, being cuddled. It felt the way she always thought it would—warm and very nice. And she did seem to fit, just about right.

Mr. Stone kissed Mary's cheek, and Mrs. Stone's, too. "Anything that's important to you is important to us, Mary," he said. "We'll get you to that audition. We'll handle it. All you have to worry about is the *dancing*."

Chapter Eight
Weird and Scary

"It looks weird in here," Mary said. Holding her dance bag tightly, she peered into the Landers Theater.

"You've been here before," Mr. Stone reminded her. "To see plays."

"It was different," Mary said. "The seats were filled with people. Everybody was dressed up."

She remembered chatting and laughing with excitement, waiting for the curtain to open.

Now the curtain was already open. But

51

the stage was empty. Mary could see all the way to the brick wall at the back. Many of the people in the audience wore leotards and tights. And they spoke in nervous whispers.

Someone was waving from the first row of seats. "There's Miss Drew," Mary said. "And Pat and Ellie and the others."

"You go on down with them," Mr. Stone said. "I'll wait for you right back here with the other parents."

Mary ran down the aisle. Miss Drew welcomed her into the group with a hug. "Excited?" she asked.

"Yes," Mary said. She was more than excited. She was *scared!*

"We all are," Miss Drew told her. "We're excited and nervous and even a little afraid."

"You, too?" asked Mary.

"Sure," said Miss Drew. "But I've already finished my audition."

"Are you going to be in the ballet, Miss Drew?" Ellie asked. She and Pat were squeezed into the same seat.

"I hope so," Miss Drew said.

"Don't you know?" Paul asked.

He and Stanley were sitting in the same seat, too. So were Nancy and Sarah. Everyone seemed to be hanging onto everyone else. There were Ballet Twos and Threes there, too. They were doing the same thing.

Rosa was alone. She scooted over and patted the other half of her chair. Mary slipped in beside her.

"The adult parts won't be announced until tomorrow," Miss Drew explained.

"I sure hope they tell us our parts tonight," Paul said.

"Me, too," Nancy agreed. "I couldn't wait until tomorrow night to find out."

"I'd tell people their parts right away," Pat said.

"That's not our job," Miss Drew said. "Our job is to dance as well as we can."

"What if we don't know the steps?" Pat asked.

"You'll know them," Miss Drew said. "They'll be the same steps you've already learned. They'll even have the same French names. You can take a ballet class anywhere in the world, and the steps and their names will always be the same."

"What if they ask us to do steps we haven't learned yet?" asked Paul.

"Then listen and watch," Miss Drew said. "They'll be explained, just the way we do it in class."

A man with a beard called Miss Drew away. The Ballet Ones, Twos, and Threes got very quiet.

"I hope she comes right back," Rosa whispered to Mary. "I hope she stays with us the whole time."

"Me, too," Mary said. She looked around. "Where's Lynn?"

"She can't audition," Rosa said. "Her parents said no."

"That's terrible," Mary said.

"I know," Rosa said. Then she put her finger to her lips and said, "Shhhhhhh!"

Mary turned around. A very tall woman with short black hair ran up the steps onto the stage. She wore a long, flowery skirt over her leotard.

Miss Drew dashed down the aisle and whispered to her students. "That's the director of the Springfield Ballet Company," she said. "Her name is Miss Kaye. She decides who plays which part."

Miss Kaye walked to the center of the stage. Mary couldn't decide if she looked nice or not. Just looking at her made Mary's heart thump.

"I'd like to see the youngest dancers first," Miss Kaye called out.

Everyone in Ballet One squealed with fright. Rosa grabbed Mary's arm. She held on so tightly it hurt.

"Ballet One!" Miss Drew said sharply. "None of that. You go right up there with the Ballet Twos. And make me proud of you."

Miss Drew nodded at Mary. Mary stood up and led the way to the stage. Her whole body was trembling.

Chapter Nine
On Stage

A crowd of children from other dancing schools joined the Ballet Ones and Twos on stage. Everyone made a circle around Miss Kaye.

"Let's do some walks and runs to warm up," said Miss Kaye. "Follow me."

Around and around in a big circle they went. They walked, marched, skipped, and galloped.

The more they moved, the less Mary trembled. But inside, she still felt nervous. So far, she could do everything Miss Kaye asked. But there was no way to know what might come up next.

"Make a straight line, please," Miss Kaye said.

Mary, Ellie, and Pat pressed themselves into place with the others. Miss Kaye looked up and down the line. Mary wondered why. Could she tell if they were good dancers just by looking at them?

For a long time, Miss Kaye didn't say a word. She just put a finger to her chin and kept on looking.

Suddenly she clapped her hands and said, "Follow me, please." She did a step she called *pas de chat*. Mary had never done it before. But Miss Kaye explained it carefully.

"It means 'step of the cat,'" she said. "It's a quick little jump, see? Doesn't that look like a cat leaping?"

It did! Mary and the others tried it. It wasn't too hard. It helped to think about the cat.

"It's a good step for mice, too," said Miss Kaye. "They're quick little jumpers, too. We need a lot of mice for this ballet."

She moved half of the children to the left side of the stage. Pat and Ellie were in that group. So were most of the other Ballet Ones. "You pretend to be mice," she said.

She moved the other half to the right side of the stage. Paul was in that group. So were the Ballet Twos. "You pretend to be soldiers," Miss Kaye said.

Ellie and Pat made faces at Mary. They didn't want to be mice. But they were lucky to be anything at all. Miss Kaye hadn't put Mary in either group! She was left all alone in the middle of the stage.

"Where do I go, Miss Kaye?" she asked.

"Stay right where you are, Mary Stone," Miss Kaye said.

How did Miss Kaye know her name? Mary wondered.

Miss Kaye showed the mice and the soldiers how to fight a make-believe battle. She seemed to forget all about Mary. *Why?* Had Mary done something wrong?

"Mary Stone," Miss Kaye said at last. "You are too tall to be a mouse, and too short to be a soldier. While the two sides fight, I want you to pretend to be afraid of them both."

Oh, no! Mary thought. I'm Mary-in-the-middle again!

But she did what Miss Kaye asked. First the mice did their *pas de chat* toward the soldiers, and the soldiers ran away. Then the soldiers marched toward the mice. And the mice ran away. Mary dashed back and forth between them.

"Look really scared, Mary," Miss Kaye called to her. "As afraid as you can be."

That wasn't hard. Mary *was* afraid! What if everyone got a part in the ballet except her?

After a while, Miss Kaye stopped the pretend battle. She had everyone do a lot of steps—*balancés* and *chaîné* turns and steps Mary didn't know.

Sometimes Miss Kaye made them dance alone. Sometimes they danced in groups of three and four and five. She moved Ellie and Pat from one group to another and back again. But she hardly paid any attention at all to Mary.

Finally Miss Kaye said, "Thank you very much, girls and boys. Wait right where you are, please."

The audition was over. Mary, Ellie, and Pat held each other's hands. They stood so still, they hardly breathed.

Miss Kaye ran down the steps. Then she talked to Miss Drew and the man with the beard.

"What's she doing?" Ellie whispered.

"I don't know," Mary said.

"I'm going to faint," Pat said.

"Don't do that," Mary warned her. "What good are dancers who faint?"

Suddenly Miss Kaye was back on stage again. She held a bunch of papers in her hand.

"Some of you will play more than one part," she said. "So listen carefully for your names from these lists." One by one, she read the ballet parts and the names of the dancers who would play them.

Pat and Ellie each got two parts. They were mice in the battle and gingerbread cookies in the magical kingdom. They gasped and hugged each other. Paul was a soldier and a gingerbread cookie. The other Ballet Ones were just mice.

Miss Kaye read the names of everyone in Ballet One and Two. Except Mary. And then, she stopped reading.

"I'd like to see the older children now," she said.

Everyone on stage raced for the steps. Miss Drew met the Ballet Ones and Twos at the bottom with open arms.

"Two parts!" Ellie squealed.

"I can't believe it!" Pat cried.

Only Mary hung back. She didn't know what to do. Why was she the only one left out? She felt terrible.

"Mary Stone!" Miss Kaye called.

"Yes?" Mary said. Her voice caught on the tears in her throat.

"I'll need you to come back tomorrow night," Miss Kaye said. Then she turned away, busy with the Ballet Threes and other dancers.

Mary looked at Miss Drew. "Why?" she asked.

Miss Drew winked. "Come back tomorrow night," she said. "You'll see."

Chapter Ten
Center Stage

Mrs. Stone drove Mary to the second audition.

"Pat and Ellie won't be there," Mary said. "Maybe I won't know *anybody*. I don't even know why *I* need to be there."

Her wobbly legs barely made it from the car to the theater.

There were only a few people in the theater this time. Most of them were grown-ups. No one was there from Ballet One except Mary.

Miss Drew hurried up the aisle to meet

her. "Miss Kaye has been asking me about you," she said. "I told her you've been working very hard in Ballet One, and that you're one of my best students."

"Thank you," Mary said.

She felt proud and nervous, both at once. Why was Miss Kaye asking about her? There was no time to find out. Miss Kaye was up on the stage, calling for everyone's attention.

"Our Sugar Plum Fairy will be Sydney Drew," she said, "director of Miss Drew's School of Dance."

Everyone clapped for Miss Drew. Mary gave her a big hug. Miss Drew was shaking a little bit, too. Mary guessed she felt proud and nervous, both at once, just like she did.

"Last night," Miss Kaye went on, "we announced most of the children's parts. Tonight, we will choose adults for the party scene. I'm also looking for someone to play Dr. Drosselmeyer, Clara's magical uncle.

And of course, we will choose Clara and the Nutcracker Prince."

Mary's stomach jumped. Of all the parts left, the only one she could play was Clara. But that was *impossible*. She looked at Miss Drew.

Miss Drew grinned down at her. Suddenly Mary knew why she'd been talking with Miss Kaye. "There are three other girls auditioning for Clara," Miss Drew said. "Just do your best."

"But I'm only in Ballet One!" Mary gasped.

"*Only* in Ballet One?" Miss Drew asked. "There's no 'only' about it. You *are* in Ballet One, and you've learned a lot. Miss Kaye asked if she could count on you to work hard and learn quickly. I told her she could. Clara is a difficult role for a young dancer. But I believe you can handle it."

Mary smiled. That's what her parents

always said, "We'll handle it." And somehow, they always did. But they never had to audition for *Clara!* She settled into a seat beside Miss Drew and tried to calm down.

The audition began. This time, grownups were called onto the stage first. And one of them was Mr. Crane! Mary couldn't believe her eyes.

"That's my teacher," Mary told Miss Drew. "Ellie and Pat and I are in his third grade."

"Miss Kaye is thinking of asking him to play Dr. Drosselmeyer," Miss Drew whispered. "He's the one who gives Clara the Nutcracker doll."

Sure enough, Mr. Crane was doing strange and spooky things on stage. Miss Kaye gave him a long, black cape to wear. He swooped it back and forth.

"Can you look mysterious?" Miss Kaye asked him.

Mr. Crane frowned until his bushy white eyebrows met on top of his nose. He made a terrible face.

"He's good at it," Miss Drew whispered to Mary.

Mary didn't know what to think. She'd never seen Mr. Crane away from school before. And now he was on stage, wearing a black cape and looking mysterious!

"Mary Stone, please come on stage," Miss Kaye called.

Mary jumped up. As she hurried toward the steps, Miss Kaye called for the three other girls to join her.

One by one, Miss Kaye asked them to stand next to Mr. Crane. First they had to curtsy to him. Then they had to waltz with him!

Mr. Crane grinned at Mary as he waltzed her around the stage. "I told you I thought this would be fun," he said.

70

Pat and Ellie will never believe this, Mary thought.

Next, a boy was called up on stage. Mary just knew he had to be the Nutcracker Prince. His name was Jeff White. He was a sixth-grader at Rountree School. And he was the handsomest boy Mary knew.

She and the other girls took turns standing beside Jeff. Miss Kaye looked at each of them for a long time. "Thank you," she said at last. "Please take a seat."

Mary almost fell into the seat next to Miss Drew. "Will it take much longer?" she asked.

"Any minute now," Miss Drew said.

But "any minute now" seemed to take hours getting there. Mary never knew being in a ballet took so much standing and sitting and waiting.

At last, Miss Kaye asked everyone who had auditioned to come up on stage. "I will

71

call your name and the part you will play," she said.

Mary couldn't help thinking of what had happened the night before. She wasn't sure she wanted to hear Miss Kaye read another list of names. But she followed Miss Drew onto the stage.

"Please stand where I ask you to," Miss Kaye went on. "We'll be taking a photograph for the newspaper."

Once again, name after name was called. Some people were told to stand on the left side of the stage. Others were told to stand on the right. The three girls who auditioned for Clara were sent to the right. But not Mary.

Miss Kaye pointed to the empty space between the two groups. "Right here," she said. "I'd like our Sugar Plum Fairy. And over here, Dr. Drosselmeyer — Mr. Norman

Crane. Next to him, Jeff White, our Nut-cracker Prince."

Mary was all alone now, at the back of the stage. Everyone turned to look at her. They were smiling. They probably feel sorry for me, she thought. She was too big to cry, but she was about to do it, anyway.

"And at center stage," Miss Kaye said, "I would like Mary Stone, who will play Clara."

Mary's mouth fell open. She was too surprised to move.

Still smiling, Miss Drew took her hand and led her to her place in line.

"Let's get set for the photograph," Miss Kaye said.

She told the Nutcracker Prince to bow to the Sugar Plum Fairy. She told Dr. Drosselmeyer to hold the Nutcracker doll as if he were giving it to Clara.

"Pretend it's the most wonderful present you've ever received, Clara," said Miss Kaye. "Look happy!"

I can handle that! Mary thought.

Her stepmother had come down to the first row and was grinning up at her. Mary started to wave.

"Hold still, everyone," the photographer called. A flashbulb went off. And another. And another.

And at center stage, right in the middle, Mary smiled and smiled.